Discover and Share

Planet Earth

Angela Royston

FRANKLIN WATTS
LONDON•SYDNEY

About this book

The **Discover and Share** series enables young readers to read about familiar topics independently. The books are designed to build on children's existing knowledge while providing new information and vocabulary. By sharing this book, either with an adult or another child, young children can learn how to access information, build word recognition skills and develop reading confidence in an enjoyable way.

Reading tips

🌐 Begin by finding out what children already know about the topic. Encourage them to talk about it and take the opportunity to introduce vocabulary specific to the topic.

🌐 Each image is explained through two levels of text. Confident readers will be able to read the higher level text independently, while emerging readers can try reading the simpler sentences.

🌐 Check for understanding of any unfamiliar words and concepts. Inexperienced readers might need you to read some or all of the text to them. Encourage children to retell the information in their own words.

🌐 After you have explored the book together, try the quiz on page 22 to see what children can remember and to encourage further discussion.

Contents

Words in **bold** are in the glossary on page 23.

Blue planet

We all live on Planet Earth. Earth is made of rock and is round, like a ball.

Blue ocean covers most of Earth's **surface**. Land covers the rest.

Clouds float in the air above the oceans and the land.

We live on
Earth. It has
land and sea.

Frozen zones

The Arctic and Antarctica are the coldest places on Earth.

The Arctic is found in the far north of the planet and Antarctica is in the far south.

Antarctica is covered by ice all year round.

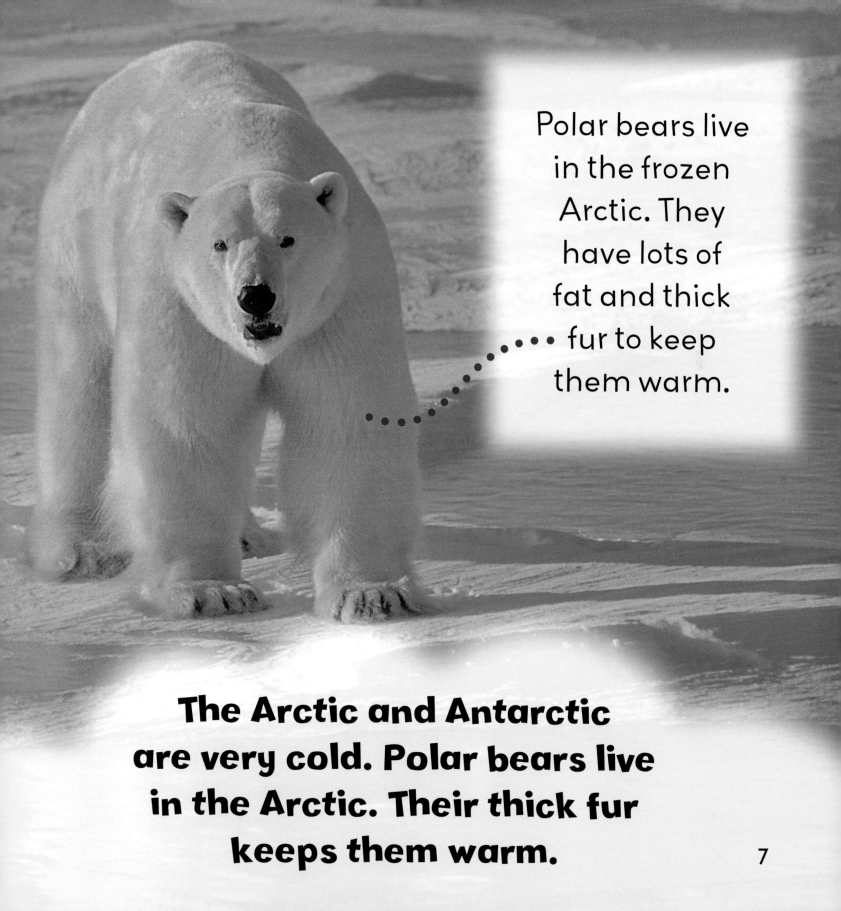

Polar bears live in the frozen Arctic. They have lots of fat and thick fur to keep them warm.

The Arctic and Antarctic are very cold. Polar bears live in the Arctic. Their thick fur keeps them warm.

7

Dry deserts

Deserts are the most dry
and **barren** places on Earth.

The ground is covered with
sand or stones.

It hardly ever rains
in a desert, but desert animals
are well **adapted** to live without much water.
Camels can survive for ten days without drinking.

Deserts are dry.
Camels can live
in the desert.
They do not have
to drink very often.

9

Rainforests

A rainforest
gets lots of rain.
Many different
animals and plants
are found
here.

It rains hard every day in a **tropical** rainforest.

Plants grow close together, and trees can grow to be very tall.

Insects buzz in the air, snakes slither along the ground and monkeys and birds chatter in the trees.

Coral reefs

The oceans are wide and deep and filled with saltwater.

Colourful **coral reefs** grow in warm, **shallow** sea close to land.

Many sea creatures live around coral reefs. They include little clown fish and big reef sharks.

Coral reefs are found in warm

sea

13

Mountains

The tops of mountains reach
high into the sky.

Some reach higher than the clouds!

A volcano is a mountain that can **erupt**.

Boiling hot runny rock called lava and hot **ash** shoot out of the top and pour down the mountainside.

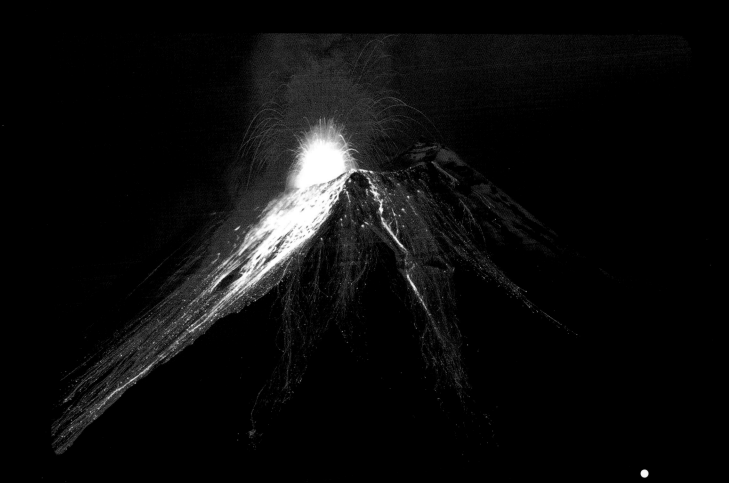

**Mountains are high hills.
Mountains called volcanoes
can erupt. Hot rock shoots out of them.**

Running rivers

A river begins as a little stream.
It gets bigger as it flows to the sea.

A river flows from hills or mountains
down towards the sea. It begins as
a small, trickling stream.

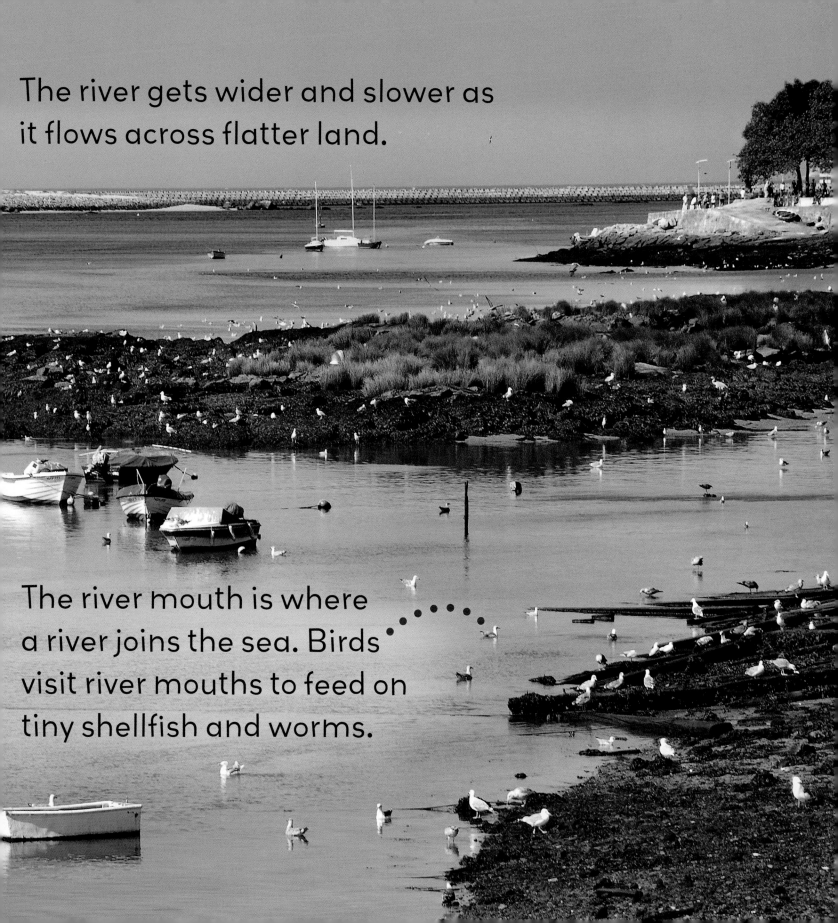

The river gets wider and slower as it flows across flatter land.

The river mouth is where a river joins the sea. Birds visit river mouths to feed on tiny shellfish and worms.

Grasslands

Grasslands are huge grassy **plains**. They are found in many places on Earth.

Giraffes, zebras, lions and other wild animals live on grasslands in Africa.

In North America, grasslands are called prairies.

Farmers grow wheat, corn and other **cereals** on the prairies.

Grasslands are big places that are covered with grass. Giraffes live on grasslands in Africa.

Where we live

Lots of people live on Earth.
Many work in towns and cities.
Cities have homes and offices.

Billions of people
live on Earth. Some
live in villages
and farms in the
countryside.

Others live and
work close together
in towns and cities.
Some people
work in offices
in very tall
buildings called
skyscrapers.

Quiz

1. What covers most of Earth's surface?

2. What keeps a polar bear warm?

3. What is a volcano?

4. What is a river mouth?

Glossary

adapted having special features that make a plant or animal able to survive in a place

ash dust and flakes that are made when something burns

barren dry and bare with few plants

cereals wheat, corn, oats and barley and other types of grass that are grown for food

coral reefs places where millions of tiny shellfish grow together

erupt when a volcano spits out hot lava and ash

plains flat, grassy land with few trees

shallow not deep

surface the outer layer of something

tropical very hot

Answers to quiz:
1. The ocean.
2. Thick fur and fat.
3. A mountain that can erupt.
4. Where a river meets the sea.

Index

First published in 2015 by
Franklin Watts
338 Euston Road
London
NW1 3BH

Franklin Watts Australia
Level 17/207 Kent Street
Sydney
NSW 2000

Copyright © Franklin Watts 2015

HB ISBN 978 1 4451 3809 1
Library ebook ISBN 978 1 4451 3808 4

Dewey number: 550

A CIP catalogue record for this book is
available from the British Library.

Series Editor: Julia Bird
Series Advisor: Karina Law
Series Design: Basement68

Picture credits: Dan Breckwoldt/Shutterstock: 21. Craig Burrows/Shutterstock: 8.
Cigdem Sean Cooper/Shutterstock: 13. Dchauy/Shutterstock: 16. Volodymyr Goinyk/
Shutterstock: 6. Pablo Hidalgo/Shutterstock: 1, 15. Jorgefelix/Dreamstime: 17. Leni
Kovaleva/Shutterstock: 4. Lluvatar/Dreamstime: 19. Loskutnikov/Shutterstock: 5. Pe
Mlynek/Dreamstime: 14. Photographerlondon/Dreamstime: 18. Howard Sandler/
Shutterstock: 3b, 11. Skypixel/Dreamstime: front cover. Szefei/Shutterstock: 10.
Turtix/Shutterstock: 20. Masa Ushioda/Alamy: 2, 12. Vibe Images/Shutterstock: 3t,
Wolfgang Zwanzger/Shutterstock: 3c, 9.

Every attempt has been made to clear copyright. Should there be any
inadvertent omission please apply to the publisher for rectification.

Printed in China

Franklin Watts is a division of
Hachette Children's Books,
an Hachette UK company.
www.hachette.co.uk